Virtue

ALSO BY HERMIONE HOBY

Neon in Daylight

interns—"Hey guys, it's time to RESIST!!!!"—and it was Jen who'd knitted one of the first of the many pink hats I saw that day. I hadn't even heard about these pink hats before I saw them. How had all the women gotten the memo? Who'd started it? Jen's sat on her head a bit lopsidedly, its nubbly ears like the nipples of some large woolen mammal. When I acknowledged her sign she made a noise like a toddler being a tiger, a fangless roar that came with a clawing gesture lifted from the sexy poptimistic videos of our early-aughts childhoods, all those writhing tan white women playing at being America's virgins/whores before they disappeared into rehab or oblivion.

"Take a picture of me!" Jen pushed her phone into my hand and held up her sign, tilting her chin down and a little to the side, doing the claw thing again and giving the camera a naughty look. She reviewed my effort on her phone then dismissed it with exasperation. (Most women my age seemed to think it their duty to berate me. I mostly didn't mind.) After a few more tries, having zipped through filters and whatever, Jen finally announced, "'Grammed!"

Zara arrived with a skinny boy and two girls, both of them noticeably taller than she was and wearing Black Lives Matter hoodies. They stood in formation behind her as though she were their tiny general while she introduced them. Zara's braids were gone. Instead, she had a short Afro that seemed to emit both self-consciousness and self-possession.

"Oh damn, girl!" Was Jen affecting an Atlantan roll? "You're serving *looks!*"

You have to remember that we were in our early twenties, basically children.

Zara's skinny friend pursed his lips and blinked theatrically at Jen, but Jen was already back on her phone, checking the Likes on her post.

I could feel a weak grin floating on my face—of white person's apology, ingratiation, exculpation—as I cast an eye from face to face, but maybe my embarrassment wasn't very interesting to Zara.

James and Amit were no-shows. Flu, we learned later, or so they said. So I turned out to be the sole male representative of the *New Old World* interns. Had I maybe misunderstood? Was the march really supposed to be just women? "Women and allies," I'd read, and I wanted to be an ally. The word made you think of rakish men with shearling jackets in World War II fighter planes.

"Ugh," Jen was saying with an eye roll that enjoyed itself too much. "I mean, trust the boys to bail."

Zara's skinny friend made an eloquent movement in the air. "Uh . . . *I'm* here?" he said, to nervous laughter. In his manifest gayness, Jen had of course discounted him, and nobody knew whether Tyler (that was his name) was truly pissed or just milking the situation for comedy.

"Let's get going," Zara said with a nod that seemed to affirm her own presence to herself.

Through the windows of the Whole Foods I could see that the streets around Union Square were teeming, a predominance of pink capping the marchers' heads—and not the soft candy-hued marshmallow shade that had become so fashionable it had acquired its own adjective, *millennial*, but a louder, less tasteful shade: Barbie pink, Pepto pink, the color of cheap toys.

We'd heard the chants from inside, but outdoors the sound was a tangible thing, something that could rise and spread through crowds and cold damp air with mass and force. Everyone around me was shouting, their voices joined in one resonant mass. "THE PEOPLE! UNITED! WILL NEVER BE DEFEATED!"

"Someone make a Kickstarter to find new chants," Zara muttered dryly.

I was embarrassed to feel moved. My eyes smarted and brimmed and I hoped neither Jen nor Zara would see. I'd never been on a march before. It had always seemed to me extreme and a bit childish to go stomping around with a sign like something out of a *Peanuts* cartoon. I'd stopped going to church after defying my mother at the age of nine, but here was a kind of church: a congregation of bodies and voices, and the joy in the chants was hymnal. I was too self-conscious to shout, but I mouthed the words. When the chant shifted, Jen began pumping her sign up and down beside me and yelling, "It's *time*! To *fight*! Nasty girls u*nite!*"

The trouble was I couldn't see Zara or her friends. "Where did they go?"

But if Jen heard me, she ignored the question.

I watched her spot someone she knew, a sorority friend maybe. The two young women squealed and hugged; "Yasssss!" they shouted at each other as indulgent marchers moved pass them. This friend also had one of the pink knitted hats—there must have been a run on pink wool.

The reunion of Jen and her friend was a kind of gift since it allowed me to drift on with the slow shuffle of so many feet, accidentally-on-purpose losing them. I didn't belong with those two; I was not a *nasty woman* in the words of the sign carried by Jen's friend. Nor did I feel inclined to try to find Zara. What use would she and her friends have for some sign-less white guy? Maybe Amit and James had made up an excuse to ditch us so they could meet up with other guys—people who were *chill*—and were marching with them instead.

Strangers smiled at me and I smiled back, bashful to be male and alone. One poker-faced bearded guy held a sign high over his head, submitting himself to the witness of iPhones: WHAT SHE SAID. Was that gallant or weak? I wasn't sure.

I myself said nothing. I had no voice. I mean that literally—I not only had no sign, no slogan, but my voice had caught in my throat. Here among so many good, committed people, with their placards and pink hats and indignation, all so brilliantly sure of what they wanted to say, I was just a guy in a cheap parka with his hood up and his hands in his pockets. I rubbed a bit of pocket lint between my fingers, punishing it into even finer granules. No one would ever write a magazine profile about me. The only epic thing about me was my student debt.

The bodies around me were almost at a standstill, and as people craned good-naturedly for signs of progress up ahead, I experimented with shuffling sideways instead of forward. Here I went, unnoticeably crablike, but there must have been a precise moment when I ceased to be a protester, because before you knew it I was standing outside a Starbucks apart from the crowds and signs and milling pink hats. Inside I joined a long line for coffee—there was an even longer line for the bathroom—amid the girls and their mothers and sisters, all joking and taking pictures and making friends. I'd always wished I'd had a sister.

Once I'd queued mutely for my muffin, I took it over to the counter by the window to consume it in squashed pinches, watching history happen outside in a slow stream of feet and voices. Middle-aged women with short hair and joy scrawled all over their faces and their arms linked. One met my eye and winked, and my face got hot. I had muffin grease on my fingers, smears on my phone screen, dust in my pockets.

Directly outside on the sidewalk a child was screaming. It was a small child in a puffy emerald green ski suit, of the sort that makes starfish out of little bodies, thrashing facedown on the ground. And the person crouching beside the child was none other than Paula, the artist, she of Paula and Jason, trying to erect a collapsible stroller, and flailing. I watched the stroller topple and Paula lunge desperately to catch it, purse slipping off her shoulder, her other hand trying to quell the kid, and I immediately abandoned my muffin leftovers and window perch and ran out to help.

"Thank you," Paula said, not looking at me; I could tell the effort it took to convey gratitude over and above her desperation. I recalled the way she'd caught me looking at her and Jason in the *New Old World* office and how she'd smiled reflexively before looking away, like a gracious celebrity accustomed to being recognized. I didn't think she'd remember me.

The kid's screams were a curdling sound and people stared with recessed sympathy or winced, throwing looks of disdain at Paula. She blew strings of blond hair out of her face, and raising her voice over the shrieking, she said, "Sorry, could you grab my purse, too?"

Obediently, I stowed the purse in the tray beneath the stroller's seat.

"Pina," she said loudly into her daughter's contorted face. "This very nice man is helping us, you see? And I really need you to get in the seat now."

The child continued to make terrible sounds until I saw something brittle snap in Paula and she spoke softly and very fast, as if conveying a threat: "If you get in the stroller right now, you can have the iPhone." The sobs shuddered down into something between a burp and a hiccup and the child ran a fist past the snail trail of snot shine on her philtrum. Paula scooped up her newly pliable offspring and buckled her into the seat.

"iPhone," the child whined, with a vibrato of self-pity.

Paula looked up at me as she delivered her phone into her daughter's grabbing hands. "You did *not* just hear me bribe my child with an electronic device."

"No," I laughed. "I mean, no judgment."

"Turns out it's kind of a dumb idea to take your three-year-old on a huge march," Paula said. "I wanted this to be a whole mother-daughter feminist moment, something for her to remember. I was all like"—Paula made stagey hand movements like someone mocking their Broadway aspirations—"*Her first march! History!* I guess three-year-olds don't exactly grasp history."

"I'm Luca, by the way."

"Oh hi, shit, sorry!—Paula." She gave my hand not a shake but a squeeze, drawing me into a cloud of orange blossom as she did. Her palm was warm and shockingly soft, and with her touch something went through me that was too intense to categorize as pleasure. It made me think of a needle penetrating the vein, its cold fluid going through you, seeping morphine and relief but, with it, that hideous sensation of a solid thing liquefying.

"And this perfect child of mine is Pina." Bashfully, she added with a little laugh: "After Bausch."

I made a mental note to google "Peena Bash."

"Hi, Pina." I peered politely down into the stroller. Her eyes now blank with concentration, her tiny hands dabbing at the screen, she ignored me supremely as only children can.

"You're getting her on a bad day." Paula looked at me. "Wait, I recognize you!" she said with a sort of prompting joy that would have been flirtatious if it weren't so earnest.

I told her where I worked—and used that verb, *worked*, rather than *interned*.

30

5

April is when those trees used to blossom in New York with their indecent smell. Jizz trees, people would say, enjoying themselves. Those trees have pretty much died out now, of course. No one I know of really mourned them; who would, with so much else to mourn? Ever since a high school English class several lifetimes ago, when a recording of T. S. Eliot reading *The Waste Land* was played and mostly ignored, I've been unable to make it through the fourth month of the year without hearing the line muttered over and over in a dour, patrician voice: *April is the cruelest month*.

That April seemed especially cruel. A seventy-four-year-old Black man was shot in the back by his white neighbor while walking on a sidewalk. He was carrying a can of Arizona iced tea. You could watch it, if you liked. Everything was caught on iPhone video. I didn't watch. There were many videos like this, and you had to choose what you watched and what you ignored. The problem was a disgusting combination of novelty and tedium: there was always another video, and it was always a bit different, but it always told you what you already knew. And you also knew that this wouldn't be the last.

I thought of how they were called news "stories," as if they were spun by some sick fuck of a Scheherazade. Maybe it was time to just let Scheherazade die, make her mortal at last.

But my big news one Saturday was that I was to meet Paula in the Union Square Greenmarket for a picnic in her studio. The days were still chilly, that damp dark shock of cold in the shade, but her arms were bare, eager for sunlight. Paula Summers summoning the summer was my impression. She was wearing tan-colored cotton men's trousers riding low on her hip bones, Pollocked all over with red and green and pink and yellow. When I was with Paula, there was pretty much no other world. She filled up every space. I thought of a paint-loaded brush dunked in water, the color flooding the jar.

In a midday excessive with sunshine, I trailed her as she skittered between stands, heaping my arms with prestigious foods. She was buying too much; I was unnerved by the note of mania in it. The smell of lilacs hit me; there were frothing buckets of them, all blowsy and oversweet, and Paula was saying, "Oh my god, Luca, let's get bunches and bunches."

"How many?" I asked, as she pushed crumpled twenties into my palm. Unpleasantly, unfortunately, I thought of a movie star pressing used Kleenex into an assistant's hand while Paula surged on to a stall where jars of honey had been stacked in ziggurats. She was walking backward now, shining at me, all her sails full: "You know that poem? Is it Rumi? About using your last coin to buy lilacs to feed your soul?"

I googled it later. It was Sa'dī, not Rumi; hyacinths, not lilacs: "Buy hyacinths to feed thy soul." Not that Paula would ever have a

I wanted them to come so everyone would know I was friends with them. How awesome would it be if Byron deigned to introduce me to Jason, only to have him sling a buddy's arm around me and say to an astonished Byron, "Oh, Luca and I are old friends."

"Well, anyway," Paula said, giving up on her fork and lifting her espresso. "I'm sure you'll have fun with or without us."

She was exuding tragedy like an expensive new perfume. What did Paula Summers possibly have to feel tragic about?

Soon after this, I excused myself for the bathroom, where I locked myself in a stall for a confrontation with my gluten-induced predicament and stared at the black-and-white tiles between my feet, dizzied by their tessellation, waiting until I heard the men at the urinal leave so I wouldn't have to meet their eyes on the way out and reveal my wretched self—the explosive shitter in stall number three. I hoped Paula would have made inroads on the cake in my absence. She had not. She was gazing out the window across the park, her fingers encircling her cup. Her nails were lambent with a shell-pink polish. She looked as though she were waiting to have her picture taken by Avedon or something, so sad and elegant that I wanted to poke her or belch. The cake slices were toppled and mushed, mostly uneaten. A waste.

"Just the check," she murmured to the waiter when he came to clear them.

It was not within the vocabulary of our relationship for me to ask her what was wrong.

"Thank you," I mumbled, as she laid her Amex Platinum in the silver dish without looking at the bill.

"Of course," she said, and it was as though her face were a piece of delicate paper I'd scrunched in a very light, perfunctory way: the annoyance was brief but I saw it. I was clueless enough back then to think that she was irritated because she always paid. Now I know that she was annoyed at the absurdity of doing otherwise.

At the subway, she told me she was going to walk in the park for a bit. I was already a few steps down and I stopped in that humid semi-darkness, with the urine scent rising from below, and looked back up at her. She was standing there, looking desolate in that dress the color of sunlight, egg yolks, and madness, like I was some bargain-basement Orpheus and she a full-price Eurydice, except we were the wrong way around, her above and me below. Still, I felt it had been a mistake to turn around.

"Oh . . . ," I said. Her face seemed to lose its bearings for a moment, and I took a tentative step back up toward her. She screwed her eyes shut and said in a desiccated voice, "Sorry."

I took one more step; now we were both standing at the mouth to the subway. People huffed past and Paula drew me out of the fray like I was an intractable kid, and then we were standing beside a vast shop-window in which a pair of unremarkable and well-lit shoes rotated slowly on a pedestal. A tiny printed card told me they cost seven hundred and ninety-nine dollars.

"What for?" I said. As if everything were fine. As if we'd had a roaring success of an afternoon.

"I'm sorry for being in such a shitty funk. Sometimes I can't . . . well, whatever. But I'm no fun to be around."

I protested gently.

"Oh, Luca, *cut it out*," she snapped, and my insides seized up for a second. "Seriously, stop being so fucking Midwestern."

"Colorado isn't the Midwest," I said quietly.

"Whatever. I'm in a shitty mood. I'm being a real bitch; don't pretend I'm not."

She must have seen me flinch, because she screwed her eyes shut again and whispered the word *sorry* several times.

I just wanted to crawl out of this moment, into some sheltered place.

"I hope . . . ," I said, faltering. "You feel better."

Paula clenched her wonky mouth in a way that made her ugly and chinny—witchy, almost—and we did a brief and sexless hug that seemed mostly elbows. There ended our failure of an afternoon.

On the subway, I asked myself what had upset her.

Now I feel like I know. Jason had made it before she did: that was the thing. This is the fact of their marriage that comes to mind when I recall this sour little outing and Paula made morose by the brilliance of the painter. My theory is that life and art had always been too mixed up for her.

She'd been dressed as a painting by the same artist on the night she met her first husband, Anton. I've retold the story to myself so many times that I feel a kind of squatter's rights about it, having tried for so long to make her story more mine than hers when she was never anyone's but her own.

This was how it went. It was the freezing New Year's Eve of 1998, and Paula and some girlfriends were at a costume party thrown by a writer in Park Slope. The host had recently won a big prize and in his great self-satisfaction was dressed as Hunter S. Thompson: bucket hat, orange aviators, toy pistol in his back pocket. Running around with his Hawaiian shirt untucked, he'd spent the night handing out Marlboros he kept accidentally crumbling between his drunk fingers, joking too often about how he should be giving out quaaludes, right? Having just been granted everything he'd ever wanted, he flashed in and out of obnoxiousness and irresistibility, eliciting both eye rolls and indulgence from his guests as Prince's "1999" played loud, on repeat.

Paula told me she'd rallied her troupe into going as paintings, and when they had all met to strategize at her friend Angelica's house, Paula had badly envied Angelica's original 1965 Yves Saint Laurent Mondrian shift dress. It was both fabulous and maddeningly perfect for the upcoming occasion. But ever-indomitable Paula bucked up and told herself she could do better, proceeding to spend days on the crafting of a white asymmetric garment, pin-tucked at the waist, with the words WILDER SHORES OF LOVE stitched in vermilion across the cloth, stretching from her rib cage all the way across her back. The night of the party the windchill was three below zero, so she wore thick black opaque tights, and over her creation, a white mink coat—a sumptuous and obscene heirloom passed down from her grandmother.

That's what Anton saw when she entered the room: a priceless coat, not the homemade and hand-splotched cotton creation beneath.

It had felt wickedly taboo to drape herself in fur, a deathly thrill, she told me. But it also put her in a state of alert; she'd think about a can of red paint volleyed from some PETA die-hard and wonder what that would do to the garment. Ruin it, obviously, but there'd also be something spectacular about it, right? If it was the right color, that is. Everything came down to color, she liked to declare. After the party, she had it expertly dry-cleaned and put away in storage before she found herself experimentally slinging paint, and so that night was the last time she wore it. Anton was wearing a bow tie. She never saw him wear such a thing again. She joked about this, like *of course* the first time you meet your spouse you're both wearing an aberration.

"How many animals died to serve you?" was his opening line

while he handed her a glass of punch as if it were a chivalrous salute. At midnight he bent to kiss her, and it was a grave sort of kiss that made Paula think, *Oh, a* man, *not a boy.* Up until then, it had only been boys. She'd felt herself to be an unserious young woman, but now here was a man with a mind that, in the ensuing weeks, revealed itself to her as some kind of vast coral reef. As he talked, she'd feel as though she were zooming out to an aerial view while simultaneously zooming in closer, drawn down into its fractal intricacies. This serious man took her seriously. This exhilarated her.

Paula was not woke, that was my generation's word, but she did have some sort of awakening: one year into her relationship with Anton she heard knuckles rapping on the passenger's-side window, jolting her literally awake. Through the car window she saw eyes as loveless as the officer's badge, and before she quite knew where she was, the cop was asking, "Ma'am, what is your relationship to this man?"

The day before, she'd watched Anton at the lectern, very in love with him but also sort of embarrassed when he paused in his brilliant thoughts and polished his glasses with his large and manicured hands before resuming. And now he was a man commanded to put those same hands "where I can see them," bullied by a guy in uniform with a gun, laying his hands on the hood of the rental car while the officer, a man of indeterminate ethnicity but not Black (how much better for the story, Paula would later think, if he'd clearly been a white guy!), peered at Anton's license and registration with skepticism. She stood on the side of the road, hands half in the air—a gesture of incomprehension as much as surrender—and in the heat of an empty highway, a high white sort of sound seemed to concentrate overhead, like a scream strafing her skull. The officer tossed the license back with an officious "Thank you, sir" and Anton said nothing.

While her future ex-husband sat in the driver's seat with his hands on the wheel, Paula stood by the side of the road watching the police car recede until it was toy-size and flickering on the horizon, then squatted in the dust and vomited her continental breakfast between her shoes. She wanted this response to be a physical reaction to racism—*I literally vomited*, she could hear herself telling a girlfriend. Except it wasn't that. Once she and Anton were back in Princeton— once she knew (eight weeks) and once she'd done what they agreed was the right thing at this time in their lives (but he agreed more)— she'd been able to explain to herself that she'd been pregnant and now she wasn't. Her body, however, seemed to reject this explanation and rose up in a revolt; she bled, her breasts swelled with useless milk, and uncontrollable crying jags gripped her for hours. The crying, which Anton received as an indictment, sent him into rages.

On the anniversary of the abortion they had a fight so bad that the only thing to do was to get married. The wedding took place in Princeton, four days after the planes hit the towers. Far too soon for any kind of celebration in America but too late to cancel, and if not now, when? So they'd had a modest ceremony, with a muffled discharge of champagne corks, and a party that died discreetly by ten p.m. with rueful hugs among the congratulations. A week after the wedding, she learned that her old lover, the finance guy, was among the unaccounted for. Paula told me it didn't seem right to her that such a winking, ridiculous fellow could have attained a tragic end and become part of history, his name eventually etched in the bronze of the memorial waterfall. But fate was weirdly indiscriminate in how it assorted character and event.

Paula ended up spending a bit more than five years as Anton's blond and vivacious young wife, and, at first, she felt she acquitted herself in

I persisted in my quest for the listenable, found *Neon Bible* and, as a grudging reserve, *Bob Dylan's Greatest Hits*. I was reviewing the CD's track listings and omissions, mentally rearranging my official position on his oeuvre, improvising a definitive ranking of the studio albums in case anyone asked—Would Jason ask? Would we argue, man to man, over whether *Desire* was better than *Blood on the Tracks*?—when a rapping came against the window. I dropped the CD with fright, the figure outside the glass jumped, too.

Zara! Her fist frozen in a second knock.

I cranked the window down. "Zee!"

I can't remember when I'd first started calling her this.

"Whoa, I did *not* think you'd react like that. You out here selling drugs or something?"

I told her I was borrowing a friend's car, which did somehow feel like a crime, though I kept that to myself. "What are *you* doing here?"

"This is my neighborhood, I live here." She indicated one of the small brownstones behind her, in a neat array behind a cast-iron fence and a jumble of trash cans.

"Oh!" I added: "Great neighborhood."

She narrowed her eyes. Zara could always tell when I or anyone else was spouting phatic rubbish, just more words on the trash heap of human speech. "Rent is too damn high," she muttered, which seemed like another reference to something. Then she leaned on the window, appraising me, her friend.

Hi, here I was.

"So where you heading, Marty McFly?"

I guess the beat-up Toyota did sort of evoke a DeLorean. But then it occurred to me that she might have been referring to my guileless-ness, my wide-eyed and witless self.

I mentioned Maine and sailing and parades.

"What white nonsense is this," she murmured, but not without warmth.

I offered her a ride to the subway and was happy and surprised when she climbed in. It felt nice to have her there beside me, a companion—a guy and a girl in a car, just like America intended. I wished it might last for longer than just a few blocks, and I even had a crazed, split-second urge to invite her with me to Maine. Maybe not even that absurd? Surely Paula and Jason had room for one more in their casually expansive hospitality. Why not bring a friend?

Because the notion of sharing them with anyone was unconscionable. They were mine.

The car's brakes made a soft mournful whine of protest, like an old dog in its sleep.

"So you're peacing out." Zara had leaned her cheek on her fist and was gazing out of the car window.

"Guess so."

"Gone the whole summer?"

"Maybe."

(Jason and Paula had been vague.)

"Huh." She turned to me after a moment. "So do you have family there in Maine or what?"

I shook my head.

"Oh, you lone-wolfing it?" I so longed to merit the tinge of respect in her question. "Off to write a novel in a cabin or something?"

"Nah," I said, though a smile crept over my face like weeds.

"Ohhhhhh!" she crowed, a touch of Raqisha to her in this moment. "Oh, this is a *girl* thing. You've got a girl up there!"

"Nope."

"Come on, I know that smile! Why you pretending?"

"No, really," I said good-naturedly. "I wish! It's these older friends of mine, this couple. Well, this family. They've got a bunch of kids. Paula Summers and Jason Frank?"

I felt shy saying their names and took my eyes off the road for a second to track her reaction.

One finely shaped eyebrow hoisted itself. "The filmmaker guy from the funeral?"

"Yeah. And Paula, his . . . wife." I stumbled on the term. It didn't seem right. But, of course, that's what she was. "She's a painter," I added. It seemed feminist to rescue her from the mere designation of *wife*. "She's actually done a bunch of *New Old World* covers." I was echoing Julia's introduction, aping her air of savoir faire, and in so doing, I falsified things.

"All right . . ." Zara's words were drawn out with singsong doubtfulness. "Well. You do you, Luca."

I hated that phrase. How to *do you* when you don't know who *you* is? And what if you did you by doing the worst thing you could possibly think of? Was that how you found out who you were?

"They're really great people," I said. She'd hurt my feelings. "What, you don't think so?"

"I don't know them," she said simply.

I could feel this fidgeting duet of tension, the static between us.

"Well," I said. "I do . . ."

"They just seem like classic bougie liberals to me. You know, they show up to a meeting at the magazine to feel good, congratulate themselves."

I said nothing.

"They're not that good, Luca."

It was as bald as that. *They're not that good.* Like their lack of suffi-cient goodness wasn't worth putting into words any more complicated than this. I don't think she meant morally, per se. She meant as human propositions, which was more comprehensive and hence worse. I felt like I'd just credulously praised a bad middlebrow movie, failing to recognize it as sentimental and cheap. Subjectivity, I decided, was a palliative for morons.

"Well," I said pointlessly. "Who is?"

"Yeah . . . ," she noncommittally conceded.

Now that we'd sunk in this moraine, failing at actual conversation, I asked her what she was up to this summer. I was not prepared for the blue flare of her attention beside me; she was tripped into hyperalert.

She told me about the activist group she was part of and the inspir-ing older women she'd met there. She talked about things needing to happen and how urgent it was, and damning statistics and uncompro-mising slogans flowed from her as smoothly as a twenty-four-hour news channel's chyron. Her fluency had all the power in our space; it was like she was no longer Zara anymore, although I knew she would have said the opposite, that this was the true her: dedicated, tunnel-visioned.

"Remember Tyler and Nicole and Lorette?" she said, breaking out of her speech into a humanly impatient question. "From the march," she prompted. "I was with them at the Women's March. They're in the group, too. Well, Tyler bounced, but Nicole and Lorette are still in. Nicole's uncle was a Black Panther."

I made the requisite noise of admiration.

"So getting his perspective on things has been key for me, espe-cially when it comes to violence."

"Violence?" I asked, as if I'd never heard of the thing.

"You know, the ethics of protest. Nonviolent versus violent. Those guys had a mission. Those guys did not mess around."

When we reached Zara's subway station, she was still talking as I pulled over and parked.

"So, yeah," she said, unbuckling her seat belt. "That's where I'm at."

I murmured something about it being awesome, her being awesome, but it came out stiffly. Who wanted to be the white dude telling the Black woman she was doing a great job while he went off to fuck around on boats with rich people by the sea?

And then there was something between us, a sort of thickening in the air I couldn't parse.

"What?" I said. She was looking at me like she was trying to make up her mind about something.

"I've also been . . . Well, I've been writing this long thing."

"Oh, that essay for *The New Old World*?" I said, with a wave of alarm, remembering how casually she'd dismissed Julia's offer at the party.

"Um, *no*." She did a quick laugh. "Definitely not for *The New Old World*. In fact, for literally anywhere but *The New Old World*."

When I asked her what it was about, she made a purposefully teasing face, eyes to the side like, *Should I tell him or not?* I knew I was meant to find this cute, and I did.

"You're being so mysterious!" I protested.

The last time I'd seen her, she'd been reading a poetry collection by a queer guy from Louisiana with a major Instagram presence. "Is it about that poet . . . I forget his name, that one you were reading."

"*Ugh*, no. I mean, they were fine, they were good poems or whatever, but *fuck* poetry, really."

I raised my palms from the wheel in surrender. I'd never heard her say *fuck* before, was the thing.

131

"I mean it. Fuck culture. Fuck all of culture."

"What?" I said, and looked at her.

She looked straight back. "I said what I said."

Maybe I *didn't* want to hear this. But I nodded at her to go ahead.

"Okay. Here's the thing. I would rather have an even semifunctioning, even halfway humane society with no culture than this . . . this, like, *barbaric* nightmare that is America right now. You know what Dostoyevsky apparently said, right? 'A pair of boots is worth all of Shakespeare.' Yeah, I feel you, Fyodor! Because imagine going up to one of those tiny kids in a cage at the border and being like, 'Oh hey, I know your parents have been ripped away from you, possibly forever, and you're freezing cold and sleeping on concrete, *but don't worry, here's some Dr. Seuss.*'"

"Well, it might distract them a bit," I mumbled. "*Dr. Seuss.*"

She let out a quick high scream, shut her eyes, and threw her head back in her seat.

"Oh, the places you *won't* go, more like!"

"I mean!" I said. "I mean, sure, we all need . . . *boots.* But what's the point of having boots without Shakespeare? I mean, isn't it Shakespeare that makes it worth it to be alive?"

"Not without fucking boots."

I was struggling.

"But it's not like it's one or the other, is it?"

"I'd do away with all of Shakespeare if it meant we'd never had slavery, never had all these illegal genocidal wars, never had, like, every sick evil of late capitalism. Did Shakespeare prevent that? Can Shakespeare fix that? Nope."

I didn't have the will to fight. (*The* Will *to fight*, I thought bleakly.)

I remembered Paula, in Union Square, misquoting the lines about spending your last coin on hyacinths. *Soul* was not a term I felt I could invoke in front of Zara. She was too empirical. And, yeah, I guess feeding your soul was a luxury. Still, didn't you need bread but also hyacinths, boots as well as Shakespeare? Shouldn't all these debates have been settled by smarter people than me long ago?

"There is no document of civilization," she said, clearly quoting something, "which is not at the same time a document of barbarism."

"Obviously," I said, sensing the gravitas of quotation.

"Walter Benjamin." She said it with the *y* sound, *Benyameen*. Another thing I'd missed.

"I just think," I said, "that maybe we can have both. That maybe . . . they help each other."

"Thanks, *Sesame Street*."

"Hey," I said.

More gently, she went on: "Well, anyway, the point is maybe I could send it to you . . . The thing I've been writing."

"Sure! I just . . ." I didn't know why she'd want to send it to me.

"To read, I mean," she said stiffly. "Before I submit it anywhere. Never mind. You got things to do. And it's probably dumb anyway."

"I'm sure it's not dumb," I said quietly.

Her hand was on the car door handle now, but she hesitated. "So you're really going for, like, five weeks or something?"

I confirmed I was. Why did I feel guilty about this?

"Well," she said. "I'll see you when you're back?"

"Yes, totally, of course!"

I leaned across the center console to give her a quick hug goodbye.

"Take care!" I called as she got out, but I don't think she heard. I edge of the pool. To wear something on the brink of ridiculous struck me, in this moment, like the working definition of style.

"So neither of them's come on to you?"

I did a small nervous laugh and shook my head.

"Do you want them to?"

I was taking a gulp of sangria as she said it.

"Oh look!" she said. "Speak of the devil."

Jason, fresh out of the pool in a pair of Guantánamo-orange shorts, was taking a chair next to her, dripping. He had a small taut gut, but his pectorals looked like they could clench and send every droplet springing off his chest, just bounce them off through sheer force like a cartoon hero. I could not imagine ever being a man who did not feel diminished by being naked. I remembered walking out of the gas station at seventeen, humiliated, clutching my jacket against my pale naked chest and its sad titties.

"Is she terrorizing you, Luca?" He poured himself a glass of sangria, raked a hand through wet hair. "She does this." He downed a couple of big gulps as though it were lemonade, Adam's apple bulging and falling, then let out a stagey smack of satisfaction.

"Only a bit," I said affably.

Bronwen bloomed into outrage. "Asking questions is being a terrorist now? If you want terrorism, look at what my fucking son's doing to that flamingo."

We turned to see Aidan simulating sex with the inflatable bird. He had all the erotic technique of a pile driver. Between titters, Noah and Eli were covertly glancing toward the parental zone, anticipating reprimand, maybe even hoping for it.

"Lively kid," Jason muttered, then caught my eye. My insides jumped at this ember of conspiracy between us. Or was I imagining it?

Bronwen stood up from her chair, cupped her hands into a mega-phone, and bellowed: "AIDAN, DO YOU WANT ME TO COME OVER THERE AND SMACK YOU?" Sullenly, Aidan flung the flamingo into the pool, where it wobbled briefly before recovering from its trauma and floating toward the shallow end.

At some point, I'd finally achieved enough sangria in my blood-stream to remove my T-shirt and get in the pool, whereupon I was instantly drawn in to adjudicating the boys' dive-bombing competi-tion. They yelled my name—competing for my attention, clamoring, "Luca, watch this, Luca, look at me, Luca!" Lacking the resolve to leave, I was stuck there standing in the water as the sun bore down on my back and shoulders.

That evening, I found myself thinking of how I would recollect these days, aware of how I was already gilding them with what felt like a strange kind of homesickness—for a place that wasn't my home, for a time I hadn't even left.

We were out on the deck and I caught the sweet herbal reek of bug spray as Paula doused her feet. They were magnificently ugly, her feet—bunioned, a jumble of callouses and gnarly toenails—and I felt winded with tenderness for them. I imagined putting my mouth around each toe, one by one, warming them, feeling the tiny scrape of each of her toenails on my palate. I had that faint feverish feeling that comes from a sunburn, hot skin all shivery after the sundown cool; Paula had given me a bottle of aloe lotion and lent me a black sweater of fine, thin cashmere, and these two things, lotion and cashmere, had put me in a sensory sort of ecstasy over my own skin.

15

W hat happens to her now?" I asked.

Paula looked up with surprise. We were outside at the table under the trees, lingering over breakfast. (That was the only verb for those mornings: you *lingered*, you squandered the luxury of the morning with cherry jam on your fingers and sun in your eyes and one more cup of coffee.) She smelled strongly of the fixative she'd sprayed all over her creation earlier that morning; it was one of those welcome chemical smells you want to huff, like gasoline or fresh paint.

"Who?" She was thumbing open an obscenely ripe fig, carmine-colored, sucking juice off her fingers, a voluptuary.

"Lady Liberty."

"Oh!" She laughed, drawing up her bare legs. There were short blond hairs on her tanned knees, silver-white in the sunlight.

"She gets burned! All the floats do. We have a big bonfire."

She offered me a torn bit of fig flesh with her fingers. I must have been staring at it. I took the fruit, mutely ate, and considered this.

"Shit gets real pagan, Luca," and she pulled a face at me, sticking out her tongue like Gene Simmons.

After all that, after those seven days of work and creation, the thing was damned to flames.

But before the later afternoon parade and the evening bonfire on the green, there was the flotilla, the big event orchestrated by Paula.

When we arrived at the harbor on the morning of the Fourth of July, there was a jolly confusion: who was in which boat, what would fit where, and someone's dog was jumping in and out of the boats, rocking the vessels as their crews squealed, the animal egged on by everyone's laughter. Bronwen, with her hands on her hips, was pulling a face of weary forbearance while other parents smiled more patiently, obeying Paula's directions. I blushed a bit when she called my name, hand cupped around her mouth: "And, Luca, you're coming with Pina and me!"

"See you guys there!" she yelled to the stragglers still fussing at the dock. Pina echoed her, a scratchy little voice yelling, "See you guys there!" as she waved. We laughed and Pina looked hurt and annoyed to be laughed at.

Paula was, naturally, an excellent rower—efficient and precise and powerful.

"You want to try?" she asked.

"Absolutely not," I said good-naturedly.

Our rowboat was one among many little seafaring vessels setting off from the boatyard, heading across the bay to a mass picnic on a spit of land. At low tide, Paula said, you could walk right across the sandbar like Jesus, over the inch or so of water that covered the path.

When we reached the barrier island, I tugged the boat up the beach; I could do that at least. A patchwork of blankets and sheets was spread on the sand, and people were unpacking food and stacks of red plastic cups and bottles of rosé. Some of the dads and kids, Jason and the boys among them, had already gotten a fire going, poking it with driftwood staffs to rile its embers into sparks.

The hot day began blackening in the early afternoon.

"Oh fuck," Paula said, frowning at a thing beyond her control. "I hope the bonfire isn't rained out later. The bonfire's the best part."

Huge and marvelous clouds were forming, great purpling banks of them that were almost comic in their drama. I felt the first drops on my skin.

"Here it comes!" shouted one of the dads, like the lead passenger on some roller coaster about to take its big dip. Then the sky opened up and it was pouring. The kids weren't even shrieking, just chattering excitedly. It was the grown-ups who made more of a fuss, sweeping up the blankets and sandy beach towels and gathering children to them with paddling motions, and soon the picnic had turned into a primordial huddling around the fire. One giggling teenage girl, a pale redhead in a pink gingham bikini, scooted under the beach towel that I held over my head and cowered there, her thin shoulders brushing my shins, freckled skin moving across the wing points of her scapulae. I forgot whom she belonged to and feared her parents would think I was some kind of perv, but I couldn't exactly *eject* her from my shelter. So I just sort of pretended she wasn't there.

The rain was violent and joyous and short-lived and then the terrible clouds rolled on beyond us and out to sea, and the fire sputtered, struggled on, and prevailed. A bearded and ruddy guy in wraparound Oakleys started gesturing with one hand and holding up his horizontal iPhone with the other. Photo! Time for a group photo! Picnic, rain-storm, fire—already the event was taking on the shine of legend. Everyone slung arms around one another and held their grins in perfect silence while pictures were taken. Several of the kids held up the sausages they'd roasted in the fire in poses of facetious triumph.

I felt some kind of contraction in my sternum of envy for these sweet, trusting, happy kids whose childhood memories would be a vivid collage of messing around in boats, the mild peril of outdoor adventure, and the sheltering ring of kindly adults. This day would be cut into a bright piece and pasted on the collage board of their memory: the flotilla to the sand spit, the dramatic rainstorm withstood, sausages (organic, local) broiled and bursting in the smoke of a drift-wood fire. Broomfield had supplied me with no childhood memories like this. Vacations had been trips to New Jersey to stay with my aunt, a woman who each year grew more obese as my mother became bonier, as if each were doing it to spite the other, a fucked-up sisterly psychodrama played out in their bodies.

The parade that afternoon entailed us towing Lady Liberty through the streets on a small trailer, up to the green, where a pyre had been built. She was one of about a dozen floats—including a large elephant and donkey high-fiving each other ("Fuck, a bipartisan fantasy," Jason had muttered)—and she was, predictably, the most spectacular. It was silly, but I felt proud.

As dusk began setting in, there were sparklers inscribing parabolas of light through the darkening air, the odd firework ripping up across the sky with a squeal and a burst. And then, when I could see Venus up there, a hot point in the cool dark sky, all the floats were dragged onto the pyre, doused with lighter fluid, and the whole mass was set ablaze while placid firemen stood by with hoses.

"There she goes!" a voice shouted in the crowd, as the flames leapt and crackled. Maybe it was the same guy who'd yelled "Here it comes" when the rain started earlier. People whooped and hollered, their faces flickering and Halloweenish in the firelight.

Jason's expression was like a slab of rock. It made my insides shift just to look at him that night. He could look scary even in quiet moments, and he and Paula had been fractious all day; I could feel the thickening barometric pressure between them, all their human weather.

As I watched the flames take to Lady Liberty's skirts like spidering hands, Jason stood beside me with Pina on his shoulders, as massive and cool as an iceberg. Paula raised her arms above her head, spread her fingers to the sky, and cheered, and it occurred to me that Jason's grumpiness might be in inverse relation to her good cheer: the colder he got, the warmer she grew.

The flames were lapping Lady Liberty's throat and cuffing her corona with fire—and it wasn't the tedious, clanging symbolism that hit me (America in flames!) but some atavistic horror. It spooked me to see a human figure burning, even one who was seven feet tall and made of papier-mâché—it gave me a bad feeling.

This image supplied by that evening of an over-freighted symbol going up in flames has since, in a dreamlike way, become confused with the other memory, the real memory of the real statue and the undeniably more significant thing that happened later on. But it's the vision of this fake one, a burning effigy, that produces in me the stronger feeling, as if sooty dead fingers were probing my chest cavity.

"All right, we done watching Liberty go up in flames?" Jason said it so testily that I saw joy snuff itself out on the faces of his sons, like flowers flinching their petals shut. It wasn't the first time the four of them reminded me of plants—as guileless, as intent on survival. Neither blame nor forgiveness was even a concept with them when it came to their dad, who at least for now, remained infallible in their eyes: their hero, builder of treehouses, baker of bread.

Back at the house, everyone shuffled off to bed instantly, done with one another and the night.

I climbed into my own bed smelling of wood smoke, a wild, romantic smell that I hoped would infuse my dreams. Whatever those dreams may have been that night—probably just the usual, showing up for the SAT when I hadn't studied—I woke up again to angry voices in the middle of the night, and this time I could hear every word, they were so loud.

"I told you I didn't want to come, and then you did that thing you always do—that passive-aggressive thing you do," Jason was saying, every word horrifically close through the walls. I felt a taint of dread that they were doing this on purpose, as if they wanted me to hear so I'd go home. But it was worse than that, they were oblivious. They'd forgotten I was here, or remembered but they didn't care. It sounded like they were outside the door, but they must have been downstairs, pacing around each other.

"Oh come on," Paula yelled. "What the fuck, Jason."

"See? You can't even admit it! I explicitly said I was not in the mood to celebrate—and actually it's not even about my mood, it's about a *fact*, and the fact is that it's fucking shameful to be American right now. Whether or not you're willing to admit—"

"I mean, do you hear yourself, Jason? Can you just hear how you're *shaming* me for giving our kids a magical day? I'm sorry, this is just absurd, pious bullshit. As if having a picnic and a bonfire with your family on a national holiday is some reprehensible act."

"Do not do that. Do not fucking *do* that. Come on, we've been through this so many times."

"I honestly don't know why asking you to participate in family life, in social life, community life, in an annual celebration, is so terribly hard for you."

"You're demanding that I be cheerful, some jolly asshole popping bottles of rosé, when the nation is going to shit? You want me to be like *Rob* in his *Oakleys* getting the goddamn group shots in? Like I should fake my way through this fucking happy time?"

"I don't care if you do."

"Well, I'm not fucking Rob and I'm not a liar, and I'm not going to lie to our kids. This is not the time for bonfires and picnics and all this hideous patriotic bullshit. I didn't even want to come this summer—I wanted to stay in New York and *do* something—"

"Oh yeah, like what for instance, Antifa dad?"

"But like always, you overrode me. Go ahead and *tend your garden* while fascism flourishes. Fucking *Kinder, Küche, Kultur.*"

I could picture the spit that might fly from his mouth, the glint of sweat on his face. How his eyes would be bulging harder, black and bright. I pulled the quilt over my head, that fey patchwork thing that smelled of damp and cedar and lavender. I was a twenty-three-year-old man going on small and frightened boy. I didn't want to hear any more. None of it had a thing to do with me, of course, but I felt guilty. It was like that time in middle school when someone trashed the boys' toilets, defacing the mirrors with some racist stuff about a South Asian teacher, and we were all brought into the gym to hear the principal deliver this grim lecture in which she called for the culprit to come forward, and I felt so agonized with guilt that I literally sat on my palms, terrified that I was about to leap up and make some wild-eyed false declaration of culpability.

"We shouldn't be here!" Jason roared.

"So why don't you just go then! Leave us here!" Paula's voice had become wobbly with tears. "Fuck off back to the city and your pious fucking protests that make you feel righteous and do fuck-all, but don't expect to drag us with you! They need a summer vacation! They need a fucking *break*! You could have gotten them fucking *trampled* at that last protest! Noah said there were police there in riot gear—you never told me that, did you?"

"Oh my *god*, the melodrama," he said. "You would have loved that, wouldn't you? Then I could be the big bad brute who got your babies trampled in this Greek tragedy. Jesus Christ, would you grow up."

"Oh sure, I'll grow up, but you . . . you *paragon* of maturity, you just keep on with your fucking *teenage delusion* of social justice! Could you take a look at where you're standing right now? In this lovely fucking big house. How about we talk about that for a moment? About the fact that you're giving me shit when it's my money that basically gets your films made."

"Oh no, Paula," he said, as though this were funny, as though he might even chuckle at the egregiousness of the insult.

"Well, look, you can't have it both ways. You can't guilt-trip me when it's my money that lets you live your life."

"Your money! Which you worked so hard for, of course."

"I mean, honestly, just fuck off back to shitty Cincinnati and your deadbeat brothers if you can't stand being happy!"

mine passed off as hers. Or if mine still existed somewhere, intact, a prototype; if she'd held on to it as the gift it was. But I was too proud, in my humility. I needed her to tell me, I needed not to have to ask. Because that was what a gift was, wasn't it? It was something given, not asked for, that's how gifts worked, she had to know that. If you had to ask, then it became a transaction, not a gift. So I said nothing. And then Noah and Eli came in protesting one another's transgressions and swiping each other, appealing to their stepmom as mediator, and I'd lost my chance at a question.

17

During that post-Dartmouth, pre–New York year at Oxford, my first real time away from home, I'd developed—*cultivated* is the more honest verb—a specific neurosis. It was the fear that my mom would die and I wouldn't know about it, and when eventually I found out, I'd realize that at the very moment when she was dying, desperately trying to reach me, I'd been engaged in something totally dissolute and degrading. These were detailed, torrid fantasies. What if she collapsed while I was yelling a stupid drinking song in a pack of overprivileged louts? Or while I was doing shots off a girl's clammy collarbone in an overcrowded college room? Or grinding with some young thing in tight shorts whose name I didn't know? Such scenarios played out in my head as though they were part of a heavy-handed movie, one that cut between my dying mother gasping in the silent kitchen and, say, me pogoing around to some bad British chart pop, glitter on my face, tongue out like a goon.

Eventually, I got over it. I'd phone my mom and there she'd be, alive on the other end, her voice weighing on me like an unwashed comforter, with all her itchy questions and intolerable stock phrases. My relief would be swiftly eclipsed by irritation; within minutes, I'd be desperate to get off the phone, cutting her off with some excuse, and I'd hang up and breathe again. What a shit I was. But I became a better son. Growing up takes men a while, or at least that's what I told myself.

In any case, my dying-mom neurosis finally came true, in a way, that August. My mom didn't die, but I was indeed aghast to find I'd been oblivious and intoxicated while something horrible happened.

One evening in late summer, the seven of us (Pina had been left at the house in the care of a pair of adoring nineteen-year-old girls) squeezed into the car.

"Call me corny, Luca," Paula teased me from the passenger's seat. (I was belted into the back seat between the twins.) "But I keep thinking, maybe you'll meet a cute girl tonight."

"Ew, Mom," said Mal.

We were headed to a square dance, one of the last of the village's annual summer events.

"The night tends to end in skinny-dipping in the lake, by the way," Paula added placidly.

"Again," said Mal firmly, expansively, like a sitcom star: "*Ew.*"

The dance was hosted by an older couple called Jilly and Mark, who'd started the tradition at their wedding party forty years ago. Their large lawn sloped down to a lake that would later turn a thrilling and much-Instagrammed violet in the dusk, while up by the house there were kegs of beer, buckets of ice bristling with bottles, and on a small stage, the band and caller—fiddles and drum and everything.

More white nonsense, Zara would have said. Everyone danced, all the kids, adults, and old people dancing together, palm to palm and arm to arm. Human beings are meant to touch one another! It was a revelation!

Out on the lawn I spun Paula, fingers around her waist, clutching her a little; it was allowable, it was part of the dance, and at the end we were half falling over, dizzy. Jason was not a jealous man, but maybe he just never thought a twenty-three-year-old kid from Colorado could possibly constitute a sexual threat. That night I shed self-consciousness—because how could anyone be self-conscious when the whole thing was so silly, when a merry man with bushy whiskers and a tambourine was calling out the steps and everyone was fucking them up, a chain of tumbling bodies building to a sort of collapse with the final musical flourish? I saw Lannie and Mal and a tangle of other kids in a pile on that plush lawn, in the throes of that distinctly tweenage, total-loss-of-control, pee-yourself, can't-breathe kind of hysteria. I missed that.

The moon was visible long before the sun set, a sliver of fingernail high up in the violet blue, and it was one of those northern evenings when it feels like the sun might never go down, still light at nine, like the sun was a little kid having too good a time to go to bed.

"Shall we be bad?" Paula said to me, all conspiratorial, when the whiskery gentleman sang out our reprieve—"Fiiiiiiive minutes, ladies and gentlemen!"—and everyone stood or lay around gasping and glowing with exertion. "And go have a smoke down by the lake?"

"Let's be bad," I said, without looking around to see if Jason saw us go.

We sat on the jetty, dangling our legs over the side above the water, with the sound of the party playing on behind us. I lit her cigarette for her, watching her lips move around it, the extravagant *mn!* of satisfaction and pleasure she made as she withdrew it between her first and second fingers, and blew out a cloud. She swung her calves forward in the air above the water and I stared at her bare feet, gnarly toes all bunioned and tan. Being alone with her was better than cigarettes, better than anything. Every time it happened, my pleasure was pulled taut to the breaking point by the knowledge that this time was finite.

"Are you having a good time, Luca?"

I thought she meant at the party and I told her it was great and I'd never square-danced before.

"No, no. I mean with us. I mean this summer."

I stared at her, dumbfounded. How could she even ask that?

She went on: "I'm worried it's been boring for you. You know, stuck with the two of us and the kids . . ."

"I . . . No! You two are . . . I mean, I'm so glad . . . so happy you asked me—"

"Okay, good." She scrunched me briefly on the shoulder, maybe just to spare me these spluttering protestations of happiness. Facing the water, she took a drag of her cigarette and shook her head in a quick, tiny way, as if dislodging something inconvenient. I picked at the damp old wood that we sat on, trying to ignore the unpleasant feeling that there was something else she wouldn't say.

"This," I began. "This is just the best summer of my life."

I felt my face turn hot. It was humiliating to care so much.

"Oh, that's sweet." She did me the courtesy of not looking at me. "That's so nice."

And then—I can't remember—did I ask or did she volunteer the story? In any case, it was probably just Paula waxing wistful with the expansive feeling that such a summer night engendered.

She said: "I know this is very daffy, and the sort of shit that drives Jason insane, but I *do* sort of think there's a cosmic pattern to things. You know?"

I nodded, with little clue what she was talking about.

"Definitely not empirical or whatever, but I do believe there's some sort of design in it all."

So I listened.

The first thing, Paula said, was that back in the mid-aughts she'd missed New York terribly. Princeton, in its manicured perfection, had struck her as a sort of Ivy League Disneyland; it drove her crazy how spotless it always was, as if each morning before dawn, some beleaguered band of indentured dwarfs trundled out to scrub every last brick, polish every plaque, trim the lawns with nail scissors, *heigh-ho, heigh-ho.*

By the late spring of 2006, Paula was pining for clamorous cocktail bars and honking cabs and the high reek of hot trash on Lower East Side streets. So when an invitation to a friend's birthday party in the city came, she maneuvered things adroitly, slipping her arms around Anton's old neck and saying: "Honey, it would make me really happy to—"

No good man could deny a woman her *happiness*, as Paula knew. He'd resented her going, and then became even more hostile when he realized that his resentment would be deemed unfair in the imaginary marital court where they both so often felt themselves arraigned. His weekends away were *work*, the obligations of prestigious guest lectures and conferences and symposia. Whereas this was just Paula running off for a weekend for her own fun in the city without him! A friend's birthday and not even *that* close a friend.

"But I've known her forever, I have to go!"

"You weren't even at her wedding," he'd said, frowning and drumming one finger lightly on the kitchen counter, which she knew to be a small signal of inordinate agitation.

"Exactly! Which is why I can't miss her fortieth!"

Characteristically, Paula won. She boarded a train to New York as a young woman again, a solo adventuress, all her colors flooding back into her. Here was her first weekend away in as long as she could remember; she'd booked herself into a tony downtown hotel, anticipating the pleasures of a white bathrobe and room-service breakfast: scrambled eggs, smoked salmon, that funny little white cap over the glass of freshly squeezed orange juice.

The friend's fortieth was a way bigger deal than she'd expected. When she typed the address of the party into Google Maps and clicked to Street View, her phone showed an unprepossessing door on an East Village street. And yet, as in one of those dreams where you discover a whole unknown room in your own house, that door turned out to be the entrance to something extraordinary, opening as it did onto a concrete corridor teeming with tropical plants, and through another, grander door—blue double doors with substantial brass knockers— she encountered real astonishment: an expansive network of glass-walled, poured-concrete-floored rooms filled with antique rugs and contemporary art, rooms that surrounded a large central courtyard shaded by a linden tree. In one corner of this courtyard, a spiral staircase led to a huge and leafy roof terrace. She'd marveled at the fact, Paula told me, that all this was hidden from the street. Like Narnia, or something!

It emerged that the place belonged to the friend's very wealthy art dealer, a man with a reputation for both impeccable art-market instincts and a temper as extravagantly bad as a Roman emperor's.

So here's Paula entering this fray alone, anxious to find someone she knows in the crowd, and a male voice says, "*Labyrinths* . . . ," and she thinks the person's talking about the house and all its corridors, the confoundment of so much ramifying space, so she says, "Isn't it wild!"

And he replies: "Oh. Yes. This place, too."

Now she actually looks at the person talking and he says, "I don't think you remember me."

"Oh my goodness," she says, sounding like her grandmother.

She's stepped through a door into a larger world she had no idea was here.

And when he says, "It's amazing to see you," his hesitation comes from the uncertainty flickering in the space between them, which he mistakenly ascribes to her still not completely recognizing him. In truth, it's her happy disbelief that she should walk in and he should be the first person there. He does one of those slow-dawning Jason smiles.

Glancing at the ring on her finger, he says: "You're married?"

"I am." And with frank courage she looks him in the eye. "Are you?"

"I am. Kids?"

"Boys. Two boys."

"Fantastic."

"You?"

He laughs: "The same. Two boys."

"Fantastic," she says, and he just keeps smiling his slow smile without taking his eyes from hers, weirdly unabashed by what his gaze is telling her.

So it's already begun. Because for the rest of the night, she knows exactly where he is in the crowd; it's like she's got this superpower of a sensory field, an infrared vision for him only, in which he appears as the one warm spot. And when she looks around to confirm his presence, she meets his gaze because his eyes are on her with plain ardor and the smile that strikes each of them is so excruciating that they both have to look away—as in, she knows that he knows that she knows that he knows; they're running a loop between and around themselves, ribboning themselves together.

When Jason got home that night, he found her website and on it her email address, then he fashioned an excuse to contact her— something about collaborating on something or other.

Paula exulted in the email and teased him later about it. The transparency of men in love!

The next day, they met in MoMA's sculpture garden, where they sat on a bench with their knees chastely kissing. Neither acknowledged the pretext that had sent them there, whatever it had been. Then they had dinner, then she missed her train, as she knew on some level she would, and then, already in the chemical madness of infatuation, she booked one more night at the hotel.

"We just talked and had sex all night and all morning," she told me now, extinguishing her cigarette unhurriedly on the edge of the dock. I heard the band swell into another dance behind us. "I was in love with him by the morning and I knew he was in love with me, too. I think we waited, like, a week to say it, of course."

I said nothing, just waited for more. People have always told me I'm a good listener. As though being a bad talker automatically makes you a good listener.

"It was the gravest shit." She turned and looked at me with what snapped at kind questions like a teenager at his parents, because this was one privilege afforded to the grieving, wasn't it, that you were allowed to be unpleasant? They seemed to have taken me at my word.

Paula said: "And you'll have to come back next summer, okay?"

The idea of doing this all again next summer was imponderable. Even imagining where we would all be a year from now seemed beyond me.

"Next summer," I said with a nod, and before I knew what was happening, Paula was embracing me, pulling me into the perfect softness of her fluffy sweater, her narrow frame tensile within my arms. Then I released her or she released me, and now she was hopping into the car by his side, his forever copilot, and I was watching their silver-blue Tesla roll away with a quick and careless double honk as I raised a heavy arm into a wave they probably didn't see.

Loss fell through me with the weight of a wave. I stood there on the steps for some moments after the car had gone, pulling my arms around myself. Paula had looked cozy doing this, as though she was luxuriating in her own warmth. I felt like a bad actor auditioning for a small part, pantomiming inadequate clothes and a sore heart.

It took me a long time to leave. My bag was packed, the beds stripped, blinds drawn, the furniture transmogrified into big ghostly lumps under white sheets, but I continued to drift from room to room like a wraith seeking absolution. I told myself that I was making sure I'd left nothing behind, but of course it felt like I was leaving everything behind. *There is nothing sadder than a summer house in September,* I thought poetically, then gagged on the untruth of it. The world is glutted with sadder things. My brilliant friend was in the intensive care unit while bleeping machines kept her nominally alive.

At last, I set off toward the beach, thinking I'd find some pebble or shell to put in my pocket and keep. As I walked, my mind conjured a shameful fiction, a counterfactual fantasy. In this version of things, Zara falls and dies instantly. The totality of the moment instantly enshrines her as an icon of a movement. I stand shoulder to shoulder with my fellow interns at her funeral, in no way ashamed by my tears. Maybe I even give a tersely beautiful speech or read a poem, and when my voice cracks, I bow my head to collect myself, feel the soft murmur of the assembled sharing in my grief.

What had really happened was messier, more awkward. No perfect completion, no enshrined anything. When she fell more than forty feet from the base of the statue to the pedestal, Zara had broken her wrist and her collarbone, and she'd fractured three ribs. Bones can be set and knit. Zara had also suffered a severe brain injury. The doctors apparently told her parents that in some cases even brain damage wasn't irreversible, but no one seemed to know. This ignorance seemed almost to congeal as a cheerful slogan among neurologists: *Ultimately, no one really knows!*

Now, walking to the beach, I realized I hadn't made my way to the beach at all but instead had semi-sleepwalked along the narrow path to Paula's shack and now here it was. I thought that I wouldn't go in but would just peer through the door and try to steal a little of her spirit. The door was padlocked and chained. Of course. The big house, the one filled with art and original midcentury-modern furniture and first editions, was left unlocked with WASPy assurance, but the wooden shack crouching among the pines, with its moth-eaten blankets and soft and forgotten Ritz crackers, *that* was locked. I jiggled the door just for the sake of it, a polite provocation, and at the rattle of the chain, several large black birds rose from a tree, like old overcoats flung in the air, beating oily wings as they cawed. Spooked, I

23

When I envision my marriage, I often think of a sturdy and blinkered cart horse, broad across the rump and haunches, a working animal. It's not that I think of Helen herself that way. Helen, my kind, lovely, solid, loving, practical, reliable, conscientious wife. Who yesterday came in from the garden, dirt on her hands, and gave me a look I've never seen before—blazing with some alarming new defiance—and said: "I'm not a trophy wife for you, Luke, I'm not your trophy of goodness."

Maybe I tell her too often that she's good, not often enough that she's beautiful. Why do these qualities still seem to me irreconcilable?

Helen *is* good, indisputably so, and that's why I chose her—and if I chose such a good woman, and she in turn chose me, then I must be a good man.

Sometimes she comes home from work with bruises and bite marks on her arms from the autistic kids she teaches. I'm jealous of them and jealous of my wife's body, of these unsettled and unsettling kids leaving their marks on my wife's flesh. It's not their fault that they can't relate or that in their distress and fear they sometimes lash out like wounded animals. Helen is pragmatic about their behavior and she'd definitely never use the phrase "like wounded animals"—that's my infelicity. Her patient forbearance awes me but also sometimes looms before me like some rock I fantasize about kicking.

We married each other out of great respect more than passion and, just like goodness and beauty, the two aren't mutually exclusive, but finding both at once is a rarity. Respect, you think, will last, because passion flares, flames, and dies; that's what it's meant to do, but isn't respect meant to endure? Having begun slowly and steadily, you assume the relationship will go on that way forever, but even cart horses are mortal. Sometimes these days, I endure this unbidden image of a gentle creature slowing and slowing, dragging its hooves as though they were shod with lead, and then its front knees buckle as if in prayer. Then its back legs. And then, you know—and it's a heavy knowledge, like a dentist's X-ray apron laid across the chest—that it's never getting up again.

At the airport the morning after the night of Paula's one a.m. intrusion, wretched at the gate, unslept, wearing the same sweatpants and sweatshirt as the night before, mouth like sawdust, eyes like sand, I hoped my plane would crash. I prayed I'd never make it to Denver. I felt I didn't deserve such a spectacular demise, but I wanted to die, like the coward I was. In my misery and bitterness I told myself that my mom would get over my death; I'd always disappointed her anyway. I wasn't meant to be a grown man, this was all a big mistake, I wasn't meant to be here. The world would do better without me.

On the runway before takeoff—the machine's mighty carbon-spewing engines trembling, sending droplets of rain wiggling laterally across the windows like sperm—I stared at a text to Paula that would not send. "I don't really know what happened but I'm sorry. Can I call you." A red exclamation point hovered beside it like a sore hangnail: Not Delivered. I kept copying and pasting and resending the message, but with no success.

I kept thinking about her, hatless and drunk, running out into the snow at two a.m.

In an unconscionable, perverse twist, I envied her for the victim-hood I'd granted her. I had wronged her. Wasn't it all very clear? Because wasn't the simple truth that there was a perpetrator and that was me, and there was a victim and that was her?

It worried me that her phone appeared to be dead. Now that it had happened to someone I knew, a young person like me, I lived within the ambient terror that *anyone* I knew could die. It was a constant possibility, any person dying at any time for any number of reasons. Had Paula slipped and fallen, immobilized with a broken ankle, and right now her lifeless hypothermic body was being discovered by a too-late stranger with a cry of shock? More likely she'd Ubered back to Brooklyn, told Jason everything in a flood of tears and shame, and a manly rage had swelled in him, and once I was back in the city, he'd show up at my door and fell me with a fist and leave me there with my nose bleeding, stunned and ashamed, perhaps pissing myself a bit in terror.

I turned my phone off, ate my peanuts, drank gin and tonics, and watched five episodes of *Modern Family* in which all the characters, kids and grown-ups both, shared an indomitable peppiness of affect.

As soon as the wheels touched down, that terrible violence—an absorbed blow—of landing, I reached for my phone, bore my thumb down into its top button hard, and willed it into functionality as we hurtled along the runway, braced, braking. Still nothing: my text remained undelivered.

For three days in Broomfield I mostly sat beside my aunt on the couch in my childhood home and endured her laughing very loudly at the antics of Disney and Pixar characters and singing along to the songs. My mother would join us, issuing a tart "No thank you" to the proffered caramels. We three adults, two middle-aged sisters and one deplorable son, watching animated movies made for children.

I also spent a lot of time in my bed, my teenage bed. In truth, I didn't actually want to be anywhere else. I didn't want to be anywhere at all, but if I had to be somewhere, my teenage bedroom was all that I deserved. I was numbed.

And then it was Christmas Day and I was sick with not hearing from them and sick with shame. I'd spent forty-eight hours in a fog, half trying to forget what had happened, half trying to make sense of it. Because what had it even been? Was what I'd done a crime, an actual crime, for which I could go to prison? I didn't even know. I was afraid to google the legal definition of sexual assault.

The more I thought about it, the more I suspected that Paula hadn't told Jason and never would. So I did something that seemed insane; I texted them both an anodyne seasonal message. Jason texted right back: "Thanks man! We're all stuffing ourselves with goose and rugelach here. P's about to lead us on a snowperson-building mission, ha. Hope you're having a good one."

A fucking *snowperson*. I could see it without seeing it: all of them crowding around Paula's creation in Prospect Park, arms raised in triumph for a photo that would form next year's holiday card, faces ruddy with the wintry air, laughing. Pina on Jason's shoulders, Lannie and Mal holding a perfect dab in unison. The snowman—I felt sure it would be a man, just call it a man—would be six feet tall and jauntily accessorized, seeming to exude a sense of humor, a cheerful awareness of its own absurdity. The stranger in the park they'd enlist to take the picture would be tickled and charmed, and he'd leave them happy, waving at this photogenic family as he called out, "Happy holidays!" Paula and her tribe were making merry, making memories.

In the weeks that followed, I'd find myself in the tiny Chinatown kitchen with a knife in my hand, lusting to draw it down the length of my forearm, not to kill myself, just a bloodletting. It makes no sense, but I wanted to make some kind of sacrifice—to bleed for Zara, to atone and scarify and purge. I never found the courage. I feared that if I actually pierced my flesh I'd feel something orgasmic and evil and it would overtake me and I'd be unable to stop myself until I'd severed arteries.

Such were the impulses of a young man who knew nothing about anything, who'd never really experienced suffering (except the suffering of knowing you haven't suffered), and who had never stopped to imagine himself as a husband and dad to two small boys.

Sometimes these days I wonder where that coffee-table book is that Paula gave me, about the painter and his seasons and his tulips. There are boxes in the garage I still haven't unpacked and probably never will.

As all parents know, having kids makes you think about death. In my case I think about what might go through my mind in those final moments before I leave my kids and everything else behind.